Siarra Jones

Skating Into Trouble

Step-by-Step series

Paul Breau

Illustrated by

John Beveridge

Published by TKI Productions, Inc.
Siarra Jones Skating Into Trouble is a work of fiction. Names, characters, businesses, places, events, locales, and incidents are either the products of the author's imagination or used in a fictitious manner. Any resemblance to actual persons, living or dead, or actual events is purely coincidental.

First paperback edition in this format 2019
Book cover design by Matthew Losiak

ISBN 978-1-9992322-1-4 (paperback)
ISBN 978-1-9992322-0-7 (electronic book)
ISBN 978-1-9992322-2-1 (audio)
TKI Productions, Inc.
www.PaulBreau.com

CONTENTS

Dedication   v

1. The Big Day   1
2. Tripping with Excitement   7
3. Bully Revealed   15
4. Chicken on Ice   23
5. Confession Time   27
6. Everything is (NOT) Fine   33
7. Knock Out   41
8. The Long Ride Home   51
9. Practice, Practice, Practice   57
10. An Angry Bull!   63
11. Suckered!   69
12. Open Eyes   75
13. A Hero Appears   83
14. Die of Fright?   91
15. Battle of the Skates   97
16. The Confrontation   109

Thank You   115
Jake Murphy and the Karate Choke   117
End Notes   125
Also by Paul Breau   127
About the Author   129

DEDICATION

For Sienna and Jenn
Thank you being the best part of my story.

Special Thanks
Charlotte Lightburn

THE BIG DAY

Have you ever had one of those days that starts off perfect, but ends up horrible? My name is Siarra Jones, I'm almost twelve years old, and this story begins with one of those days. Before I knew what had hit me, I found myself skating into trouble.

As I said, things started off great. I had a new skating outfit and was admiring it in front of my big bedroom mirror.

I swished my long auburn ponytail back and forth, side to side. "Not bad," I said to my reflection—and actually meant it.

I was wearing a white, long-sleeve shirt with tie-dyed pants and long socks. The pants were hand-me-downs from my cousin, but I didn't mind. They were new to me. And they looked brand new, too.

The socks had pictures of little pandas on them, and they were the cutest things you've ever seen. My best friend, Mia, gave them to me at my birthday party last year. We went to a trampoline park (so much fun), and all my friends were there.

"Come on, Siarra!" Dad called from the front hall. "It's time to go"

Hmm. My bedroom was still messy. I was *supposed* to have cleaned it up earlier, but I got distracted and read comic books instead. Priorities, right? Besides, it wasn't *really* messy, more . . . cluttered. All my dirty clothes were tossed on the floor instead of in the laundry basket. Bad habit, I know.

But I was too excited to worry about my messy room right now and I didn't want to be late.

"Coming, Dad!" I replied and ran down the stairs. I grabbed my jacket off its hook and caught up to Dad on his way to the garage.

I hopped into the car and slammed the door way too hard. "I can't wait to meet my new skating instructor!"

"Then let's not keep her waiting," Dad said as he started the car.

To say I loved skating would be an understatement. Actually, it would probably be the biggest understatement in the universe. I *adored* skating—loved everything about it. The sound of noisy kids as they rushed in and out of the sports centre. The feeling as I tightly laced up my skates. The smell of cold air when I entered the rink.

But my favorite part was taking that first glide onto the ice.

I beamed at Dad. "This class is going to be extra special."

"Why is that? Did they get a new Zamboni?"

I rolled my eyes. *Dad Joke Alert!* He knew exactly why it was special. I'd talked about it for WEEKS!

"First of all"—I glared at him—"Mia is going to be there. And second of all, you and Mom said if I passed this level you'd sign me up for our new teacher's skating camp. Jill used to skate in the Olympics, you know!"

He chuckled. "I know, I know! I've heard!"

Dad liked to tease me, but he was happy I was learning to skate. And he was well aware of my passion for Olympic skating. Ice dance, pairs skating, speed skating—I loved it all.

I loved everything that happened on the ice, except hockey. Hockey wasn't for me. Too aggressive.

"Come on, Dad, I don't want to be late."

"Right! We mustn't keep Jill waiting! Tally ho, and off we go! To the rink!"

I shook my head as he pulled out of the garage. My dad loved embarrassing me. But it didn't matter—nothing was going to ruin this day.

Once we hit the road, Dad turned on the radio and sang along to the pop music like he always did.

And, as always, I yelled at him to stop. "Dad, you sound terrible! Turn up the music!"

"I can't help myself!" He sang the words like an opera singer. "I have a song in my heart!"

"Well, it sounds like a fart!"

"HOW RUDE!" he declared, then turned up the music.

Then we both giggled and proceeded to sing along with the radio together.

This was our routine and I loved every second of it. I couldn't tell you when or how we started it, but it was always the same. And to be totally honest, Dad and I both knew that he was a horrible singer.

Thankfully, I got Mom's singing talent.

It usually took us about five songs to get to the sports center, but today it felt like it took forever. It was weird how time seemed to slow down like that. Whenever I was waiting to do something I loved, like skating, it took FOREVER. But when I was actually skating, time sped up. Fun stuff was over in a flash.

And don't even get me started on what happened during math class. I swear the clock in Mr. Carter's class stopped as soon as I opened my textbook.

We finally pulled into the parking lot, and Dad found the closest parking spot.

I was waiting impatiently by the trunk before Dad had even unbuckled his seatbelt.

"Someone's excited," he said as he popped open the trunk. "Have fun, love."

"I'll see you in there!" I grabbed my skating bag and ran ahead, smiling from ear to ear, eager to get on the ice.

But, as I would soon discover, life has a funny way of pulling the ice out from under you.

2

TRIPPING WITH EXCITEMENT

I ran toward the doors of the skating rink like a spy infiltrating into a top secret building. I zigged and zagged, dodging all the people walking to and from the entrance. To an outsider, this may have seemed a bit weird, but I've been playing this game since I was a little kid, and I wasn't going to stop now.

Come on, Siarra! You've got this!

My timing needed to be perfect: Too fast, I'd hit the doors and trigger the alarm. Too slow, I'd be crushed by the automatic door defense system. Instant death.

Okay, here I go.

Dodge the old lady!

Avoid the screaming kids!

Wait for it . . .

Now!

The motion sensor doors opened and I slipped inside. As always, I'd timed it perfectly.

"Coming through!" I yelled, bobbing and weaving between more people.

The sports center was a huge complex that contains a pool, a gym, a library, and the skating rink, and all kinds of people were hurrying to and fro. Parents pushing babies in strollers, kids in wet bathing suits with goggles on top of their heads, seniors heading to the library. And, as the saying goes, I knew this place like the back of my hand.

I ran down the hall past the pool, took the first left, and raced down the stairs to the skating rink area.

BOOM. There it was. That strange and wonderful cold-air smell. I took a deep inhale, then glanced around.

The lobby at the rink entrance was packed. An absolute jungle, with people acting like wild animals. There were five long benches with small cubbies underneath where skaters could store their regular shoes. Everyone was desperate to find enough space to lace or unlace skates and juggle equipment. Kids bumped and banged into each other at every turn. Frantic parents searched for lost gloves, mittens, and boots as the sound of screaming kids pierced the cold air.

There. Near the end of the long bench. A teenager had just finished up. This could be my chance . . .

I dodged a particularly large hockey bag and made a run for it, getting there seconds before another kid.

"Sorry." I said with a shrug, and the boy slunk away, defeated. I felt a twinge of guilt, but what could I do? This place was primitive. It was survival of the fittest. Or in this case, the fastest.

I edged my way onto the bench, staking my claim, then glanced up to see Dad pushing his way over to me. I took out my skates, gloves, and helmet.

"You can barely move in this place," Dad complained when he reached me.

I handed him my boots, and he tucked them into the empty skating bag. Then I loosened the laces on my skates and put them on. They always felt weird at first. Sometimes it felt like I'd never get my feet inside. Then, magically, they slid in and everything felt right.

"Let me know if you need any help, love."

"Thanks, Dad. I'm good."

He smiled weakly. "Okay."

Dad had taught me how to properly tie my skates the year before, but I was pretty sure he secretly missed helping me. Now that I could tie them myself, though, there was no going back. It felt really good. Plus, it was the only way to make sure they were tied exactly how I liked them. Tight. And I mean *really, really* tight.

I laced them all the way up, wrapped the laces around the top twice, and pulled them as tight as I could. Some kids tied their skates in a double knot, but I only did mine in a single. It made taking them off that much quicker so I could get out of the lobby area the fastest.

"Have a great class," Dad said. He kissed me on the head.

"Bye, Dad." I waved to him as he walked into the viewing area.

Dad always stayed to watch me skate during my lessons. He'd never learned to skate as a kid, so he was extra proud of me. In fact, he was almost as excited to *watch* me skate as I was to skate. I kept telling him to sign up for the adult lessons, but so far, he hadn't done it.

There was a routine to starting a new skating class. First, you found your place on the bench. Check. Then, you put on your skates. Check. So now it was time to grab my helmet and gloves and head over to the big bulletin board. Check, check, check.

The board was where your future was determined.

Would you get a good instructor or a mean instructor? Would you be with your friends?

Every kid in skating lessons had to find a sticker with their name on it. The names were written in different colors, and each color represented a different instructor. So if your name was written in red, your teacher was Hardeep. And if your name was written in blue, you were with Jason.

I worked my way up to the front of the big bulletin board and looked for my name. Mia and I had arranged to be in Jill's class . . . *Yes!* There it was, Siarra Jones, written in forest green. I peeled the sticker off and put it on the front of my helmet, on top of all the old stickers. I must've had at least five—they were like badges of honor.

But this was going to be the best class ever, because once I passed this level, I got to enroll in Jill's advanced figure skating camp. *Please, please, please!* I've never wanted something so bad.

I pushed through the arena doors and joined a group of kids standing at the rink entrance.

"Siarra!"

I turned around and saw my best friend skittering toward me. (Mia moves really fast, but she takes tiny steps. I can recognize her walk from a mile away.) As always, her perfectly straight shoulder-length black hair looked amazing. It was so shiny, I wanted to reach out and touch it.

Mia and I have a lot in common. We both love reading, acting silly, and singing, and we both hate hockey. She's also practically my next-door neighbor. Well, half the time anyway. Her parents got divorced last year and now she spends one week with her mom and the next with her dad at an apartment nearby. It isn't like it used to be, but it isn't too bad—we actually get to have more sleepovers. (But we like to call them *no-sleep*-overs.)

"Mia!" I said, giving her a giant bear hug.

Then she kicked off our special routine: "Oh, Siarra, I've missed you *so* much! How long has it been?"

"*Why* . . . we haven't seen each other since . . . since . . ."

"YESTERDAY!" we yelled together, then burst out laughing.

"Jill's class is going to be great!" I said.

"I know, I can't wait."

"Green Stickers!" a woman's voice called out. "Can I have all skaters with green stickers please follow me!"

Everyone with a green sticker came to attention.

Mia and I smiled at each other. "This is it," I said, hopping up and down on my skates, barely able to contain my excitement.

Jill was exactly what I'd expected. She was tall and fit, and wore black tights and a beautiful red bomber jacket. Her skates were covered in glitter—like a figure skater you'd see on TV—and her long, curly brown hair bounced as she skated over.

"My name is Jill, and I'll be your instructor for this session. Please follow me."

The green stickers all shuffled toward the ice. I counted ten of us in total.

"Hurry up," said someone behind me. "Why are you so slow? Get out of the way."

I felt a hard shove, then stumbled forward and fell.

3

BULLY REVEALED

As I picked myself up off the ground, I glanced around to see who'd pushed me. *Impossible.* I was surrounded by a sea of legs and skates. One thing was for sure, though. I would never forget that voice.

When I made it to the rink entrance, Mia was already on the ice. Darn. She must've missed the whole shoving episode. And if anyone else knew who did it, they weren't saying anything to me.

Ugh, I thought. *Kids.*

I dusted myself off and joined my group on the ice, doing my best to put the incident out of my mind.

As we skated around, Jill went around to each student and introduced herself. She was an absolutely *amazing* skater, and anyone watching would be able to tell she was a professional. Her legs were long and

15

powerful, and whenever she pushed off, her muscles flexed like they were going to burst out of her leggings.

But when she skated up to me—with that perfect posture!—I was so nervous that I couldn't speak. I stared down at the ice.

"And what's your name?" Jill asked.

I froze. It was the strangest feeling, my mouth not doing what my brain was telling it to do. If this were a cartoon, my jaw would have dropped and hit the rink. *Come on, Siarra! Don't just stand there like a dummy. Say something!*

I said nothing. And trust me, shyness was *not* my natural state. But for some reason, I couldn't even bring myself to look her in the eye.

She tried again. "You look like a strong skater. What's your name?"

Thankfully, Mia skated up and saved me from myself. "Her name's Siarra. She's usually way chattier. In fact, sometimes I can't get her to stop talk—"

I poked her in the ribs before she could finish embarrassing me.

"Ouch!" Mia said, rubbing her side.

Jill's blue eyes sparkled. "Well, we'll have plenty of time to get to know one another on the ice." She started spinning in perfect 360s right in front of me—so fast I couldn't even count how many she did—then swooshed to a stop and winked. "Very nice to meet you, Siarra."

I stared after her as she skated away. *Siarra.* My name never sounded so sweet. If only I could have said something and not acted like a complete weirdo.

Mia grabbed my arm. "Wakey-wakey. What's up with you today?" She laughed and skated back to her own area.

What was up with me today?

Maybe I was nervous because Jill was such a good skater. I wanted to impress her. I wanted her to like me. Was that weird?

After the introductions, Jill gave a quick demonstration. Frontward. Backward. Two legs. One leg. She leaped high into the air and touched back down on the ice as if weightless. She even showed us some spinning moves.

She made everything look so easy. Totally effortless. And she was fast. Whenever she stopped, ice flew high up into the air like a rooster's tail.

Jill led the class through some simple warm-ups. Bubbles forward and bubbles backward. You slide your skates wide apart, then bring them back together. Silly name, but from high above, I guess it could look like bubbles.

"Nice job everyone," Jill said. "I'm getting a better idea of everyone's skill level."

Bubbles are really easy, and everyone was able to do them. There were a couple of outliers, but most of the skaters were at a similar skill level, which is a good thing. It stinks when one or two kids are way worse than everyone else.

So far, so good.

Next, Jill created an obstacle course with small orange cones. The objective was to skate through the course on one leg, switching legs at each cone. It was a lot harder than it sounds.

I took my place in line behind a younger girl. *She's pretty good*, I thought as I watched her skate. She forgot to switch legs on a couple of turns, but that wasn't a big deal.

Now it was my turn. I took a deep breath and put my skates into a T position. "You've got this," I whispered to myself, then pushed off.

Easy-peasy! I glided up to the first cone, switched legs, and pushed off again. I was a little wobbly on the second cone, but I still made it.

As I came up to the third cone, a voice behind me growled, "Get out of the way! Why are you going SO SLOW?" I recognized the voice immediately—it was the same one I'd heard seconds before someone shoved me.

My stomach flipped—it felt like a million butterflies were trying to escape from my tummy—and I lost my concentration and almost fell down.

When I stopped to get my bearings, a tall boy wearing a hockey jersey and a helmet with skulls painted on it skated right past me. He narrowed his eyes and sneered as he went by. I didn't recognize him.

"What a jerk," I mumbled.

I watched him skate toward the end of the course. He was fast, but he had no control—his arms flailed all over the place and he didn't switch feet like Jill had asked. Plus, when he got to the end, he didn't stop. The other skaters had to scramble out of his way while he ran right into the boards.

I looked over to see if he'd get into trouble, but Jill hadn't even noticed. The kids who'd skated before us were talking with her, stealing her attention.

What a rip-off!

And because we'd been too far away, no one else heard what he'd said to me.

Feeling defeated, I pushed off and continued skating. I was upset, but the next skater was waiting for me to finish and Jill and the others were skating back to the starting line to go through the course again. I didn't want to hold up the class.

At least the boy in the hockey jersey wouldn't be behind me on the next turn.

You should tell Jill, I thought, but quickly reconsidered. I didn't want my first real conversation with her to be me telling on some jerk boy. It just didn't feel right. Besides, I could handle rude words.

And when you were a kid, it was hard to talk to adults about this kind of stuff. Who wanted to get a reputation as a tattletale?

Not me, that's for sure.

So I let it go.

4

CHICKEN ON ICE

After joining the other kids back at the start, I watched as each one skated through the course for a second time. Once again, the boy skated as fast as he could without following instructions.

The rest of the class tried to do what Jill asked.

Soon, it was my turn again. And this time, I did much better. (Um, *yeah*. Maybe because I didn't have some big jerk yelling at me from behind.)

Jill skated over to me. "Siarra, nicely done. You have good form."

"Thanks," I mumbled, not yet able to fully speak up.

But still, our first real conversation! And my jaw didn't hit the ground this time. *Phew! I'm making progress.*

This whole skating thing was starting to feel good again.

Jill took a minute to show everyone the proper way to do a crossover, then split the class into two groups of five. Thankfully, the mean boy was in the other group.

Each group skated over to their own red circle. In hockey they were called face-off circles because they were where hockey players faced-off against each other when they dropped the puck. Original name, right?

I'd watched Jill's crossover demonstration very closely, and I practiced slowly and carefully, getting better each time. Mia did too.

Crossovers were a technique skaters used to move faster around corners. With each stride, you crossed the outside skate up and over the skate that was on the inside of the curve. Believe me, proper crossovers were TOUGH—it was hard to keep your balance, and a couple of kids fell.

I glanced over at the other group and got angry all over again.

The boy wasn't even doing proper crossovers—he was just skating as fast as he could! No technique!

What should I call him? Jerk? Dummy? Fart Face?

I had a lot of options to choose from. Too many in fact.

Jill was busy helping one of the kids in our group, so she didn't notice when the mean boy skated up to a smaller boy and whispered something in his ear. Even though I couldn't hear what he was saying, I was sure it was something nasty, because the kid almost fell.

I gasped and almost lost my own balance, but regained my footing just as Jill blew the whistle.

Our first class, over already. We skated over to the exit, and no surprise, the bully was the first kid off the ice. I certainly wouldn't be racing to the change area today.

"See you next week," Jill said, high-fiving each student as they left the rink. She smiled at me when I reached her. "Good work today, Siarra."

"Thanks." I was tempted to tell her about the boy, but I totally chickened out. I guess I just wanted her to like me.

Mia and I walked to the change area together, me walking just a little bit slower than normal.

"Did you see that big jerk who skated like a madman?" I asked.

"Which one? A lot of those kids were out of control."

I sighed. "Never mind. It was a fun class, so I guess it doesn't really matter." There was no point talking about it with Mia if she didn't actually see anything happen.

Besides, maybe he'd be better behaved next week.

5

CONFESSION TIME

At last the day arrived.

Seriously, having to wait a whole week until my next lesson was just plain cruel. Skating was all I could think about.

There was never a question about who would take me to the lesson. Mom always did the laundry and took me to Girl Scouts. Dad always did the vacuuming and took me to skating.

Dad and I said goodbye to Mom and followed our usual routine in the car. But I was preoccupied. I couldn't wait to get back on the ice and work on my crossovers. Yeah, you could say I was anxious . . . the good kind.

When we arrived at the rink, Dad parked the car and

I grabbed my gear and raced ahead. Inside, I grabbed an open spot on a bench and laced up my skates.

"Hey, Siarra," Mia said, squeezing onto the bench beside me. "How's it going?"

"Great! I'm excited to work with Jill again. She's amazing."

"Yeah, she's pretty awesome. Are you actually going to speak to her today?"

"Ha, ha, ha." I gave Mia a pursed-lip face and my best Southern accent. "How very *droll* . . ."

Mia giggled at my performance.

After we finished putting on our skates and gear, we headed over to the rink. Walking on skates was always a blast because you instantly became taller. I was pretty tall to begin with, but on skates, I felt really tall. It put me in a great mood.

But then I saw him—*the skating bully*—and I instantly felt a knot in my stomach. Now I was anxious for all the wrong reasons. Lousy reasons.

He even looked like a mean kid. He wore ripped jeans, a winter jacket—and that helmet with the creepy hand-painted skulls on it.

I took a deep breath and listened to my internal voice. *It's okay, Siarra. You've got this!*

Confession time. Ever since kindergarten, I've talked to myself. Weird, right? And considering I'm almost twelve, I've been doing it for a long time.

I wasn't a fan of kindergarten. Truth is, I absolutely *hated* it. Not all of it of course—only the part from the first bell until about one minute before the end of the day. And maybe one or two seconds in between.

Life at home with Mom and Dad was always super fun. But when Monday came around? Yuck! I don't know why I didn't have any friends back then, but I was really lonely. It was hard.

So to survive school, I made up little songs to cheer myself up. I sang them in my head and they would always make me feel better. One of them went like this:

Siarra in the winter.

Siarra in the spring.

I love Siarra

When she sings, sings, sings.

Siarra in the summer.

Siarra in the fall.

I love Siarra

The most of all.

Silly, right? Come on, I was a "kindie" back then, not even in first grade yet! What do you expect?

Anyway, one day I started talking to myself as well, but only with my internal voice. I'd talk as if I were a superhero or a spy or some other more interesting version of myself. It was never like I was talking to a separate person; it was more like playing pretend. And somehow it always made me feel better.

If I was afraid, I'd pretend to be someone brave. If I was bored, I'd pretend to be someone exciting. And whenever I felt a little bit anxious or scared, I would say, *It's okay, Siarra. You've got this.*

I decided it was a good time to say it again. "You've got this," I whispered to myself.

Mia heard me and gave me a confused look.

"I mean, it's going to be a great class," I said, plastering on a smile.

She nodded and smiled back.

Phew. Good cover. I didn't want to totally weird out my best friend.

I was sure she would understand—she's good like that, we both are—but I still wasn't sure it was worth talking about. And if it wasn't, I didn't want to make a big deal out of it. Maybe today would be better?

Mia hopped onto the ice, and I watched her skate over to our classmates. She was always going on about how I was the better athlete, but she shouldn't sell herself short. She was becoming a pretty good skater.

I stared at the bully, then took another deep breath. *Don't let him get to you. Ignore him.* That was what people always said. But did it ever actually work? Somehow I didn't think so.

I held onto the boards and eased myself onto the ice. Was it slipperier today? Nah, I was just nervous.

I stood up, steadied myself, and pushed off.

There. See? Nothing to it.

I skated toward the group.

For real, Siarra. You've got this.

I didn't though. Not by a long shot.

6

EVERYTHING IS (NOT) FINE

I skated up to the group and stopped next to Mia.

"Hi Siarra," Jill said. Her smile made me feel much better.

I looked over at the mean boy. He hadn't even noticed me. *Perfect.*

Staying close to Mia, I sang a little song in my head for comfort, a different one this time:

On sunny days
or moon-lit nights,
everything will be all right.

Once the stragglers arrived, Jill separated the class into two groups again. Mia and I were in the same group, and the mean boy was in the other.

"Crossovers," Jill said. "Let's see them."

I picked a spot on my group's red circle, and we all skated around it, practicing our crossovers.

Occasionally, I glanced over at the other group. And sure enough, every time I looked over, the mean boy was skating really fast and out of control. Clearly he didn't care about anyone but himself!

When Jill skated over to speak with him, I pretended dramatic music was playing in the background. Finally! *Justice*. Now I could focus on my own skating.

Well . . . not exactly.

I waited for him to get in trouble. I *wanted* him to get in trouble. But he didn't. Jill didn't even raise her voice. No justice. Nothing.

Jill just talked to him calmly, then showed him how to do proper crossovers.

What was going on? This jerk behaved badly, and now he was getting extra attention? I tried not to be jealous. I failed. I was *totally* jealous. I tried not to be angry. I failed. I was TOTALLY angry!

My only consolation was that the boy continued to mess up his crossovers. Whatever Jill told him wasn't sinking in, and as soon as she left to help someone in our group, he went back to his old ways—skating fast and out of control.

Our group was the opposite. Everyone, especially Mia and I, wanted to get better at crossovers. We all listened to every word Jill said, then tried to do the exercises exactly the way she showed us.

It just made sense. Jill was an amazing skater. She knew how to do perfect crossovers. Why *wouldn't* you listen to her and follow her instructions? But apparently some people, especially a certain bully, weren't interested in learning how to do proper crossovers.

With about five minutes left in the class, Jill called everyone over. "Okay, skaters. We're going to play some freeze tag."

We all cheered. Who wouldn't? Freeze tag was awesome.

Jill asked which student wanted to be "it," and a bunch of hands shot into the air. "Okay, everyone," she said and pointed to the mean boy. "Oliver is going to be 'it.' "

Oliver. So THAT was his name. It was the first time I'd ever heard it said out loud. It sounded like *olives* . . . But I loved olives! Great. Just great. From now on, every time I saw an olive, I'd think of Oliver and my stomach would turn. I'd never get to eat olives again. *What a rip-off! Argh.*

The name did suit him, though. Olives had a hard pit and tasted kind of bitter. *Oliver* . . . I laughed to myself. *A boy with a hard head and a bitter attitude.*

Oliver also sounded like all-liver.

Blech! I HATED liver. I hated mean people too. Oliver was mean. Did that mean I hated Oliver?

Mom said people were usually mean for a reason, so I know what she'd say if she were here. She'd suggest I put myself in his shoes for a minute (or skates in this case). She'd wonder if maybe his parents were mean. Or if his brothers and sisters picked on him. Or whether he didn't have any friends.

Well, sorry, Mom, but I couldn't do that right now. Besides, maybe Oliver would have more friends if he weren't so mean.

Jill blew her whistle and we all scattered. We didn't use the whole rink, though—our class had one section at the end. We had to stay on one side of the big blue line.

I knew the blue lines were very important in hockey, but I didn't know much about how the game worked. Hockey bored me. Players skating around and smashing into one another while trying to shoot a puck into a net? Nope. Not my thing. The only thing I liked about hockey was the way they stopped.

It was funny, but one of my figure skating goals was to learn how to do a proper hockey stop. It was one of the things Jill's skating camp focused on, and one of the things I'd need to learn in order to pass this class.

Oliver took being "it" very seriously; he skated all

over the rink like a madman, tagging people left and right. Soon, there were only three of us left unfrozen— me, Mia, and another boy. When you were frozen in freeze tag, you always tried to get a free player to come and tag you so you could be free again. Unfortunately, most people focused on keeping themselves safe. But I liked to unfreeze people, because when *I* was frozen, I wanted someone to free me.

As I skated toward one of the frozen kids, Oliver skated toward me, fast. I stayed focused, but Oliver was gaining on me.

I was seconds away from completing my mission when Oliver came up behind me.

I'll just unfreeze the boy and make a sharp left turn to get away—

"Tag!" Oliver screamed as he shoved my shoulder.

I made a hard left and came to a stop.

Oliver skated up to me and smirked. Then, with his back to everyone else, he said, "You're SLOW."

I struggled to think of a witty reply but couldn't. This kid was good. Apparently I was dealing with an experienced bully.

Oliver turned around and skated toward another kid.

I stood there frozen, in more ways than one.

Only this time I didn't have butterflies in my stomach. My hands were clenched into fists inside my mittens. My face was hot. I wasn't anxious—I was angry.

But, before I could do anything about it, Jill ended the game and it was time to go home. I took three deep breaths.

One.

Two.

Three.

Deep breathing always helped calm me down.

When I finished, I skated toward the exit. Oliver was long gone by the time I reached the door.

On the ride home Dad cracked some jokes, but when I didn't laugh, he went quiet.

"How did the lesson go?" he asked.

"Fine."

Whenever I use the word "fine," it almost always means that things are anything but. And I think Dad knew it.

He glanced over at me. "Everything okay, honey?"

"Yeah. Everything is fine."

I was still processing my emotions. I didn't know exactly how I felt, but I knew I wasn't ready to talk to Dad (or anyone else) about the bullying.

Dad didn't ask again. He must have picked up on my signals that I didn't want to talk. Not that it was hard. A Martian would be able to tell that I was angry. Dad was usually pretty good at giving me my space, and just then, I needed it. I needed time to think about what had happened. Time to think about why this boy, Oliver, made me so mad. I didn't want to get mad, but I couldn't help it. What was it about mean kids? It was like they knew exactly how to push the *wrong* buttons.

But I was determined that the next week would be different. I'd be ready for him. I wouldn't let him get to me and I wouldn't get mad.

I decide how I react! I'M in control, not him!

For the rest of the ride home, I imagined Oliver smashing into the boards face first. *Take that!* But after a while, I started to feel ashamed. That wasn't the real me. That wasn't who I was.

When we got out of the car, Dad gave me a knowing look. But I still wasn't ready to talk.

Usually I couldn't *stop* talking. But now that something really lousy happened, something that I *should* talk about, I clammed up. I couldn't find the words or the energy to talk to anyone. Not my dad. Not even Mia.

Why was I so weird?

7

KNOCK OUT

Once we finished the next class, we'd be at the halfway mark.

I was determined not to let Oliver upset me again, so throughout the week I imagined hundreds of situations between us where he would say something mean but I wouldn't react. Believe me, the things he said and did in my mind were much worse than anything in real life. I was amazed I was able to come up with some of them.

I also replayed our meeting over and over in my mind, but each time his words rang in my ears, I would come back with a smarter answer.

Oliver: "Why are you so slow?"

Me: "Why are you so dumb?"

Oliver: "Why are you so slow?"

Me: "Why are you so ugly?"

Oliver: "Why are you so slow?"

Me: "Because your breath smells like dog poop!"

I couldn't believe how anxious I was for the next class to arrive.

When it finally did, I put my gear on and marched onto the ice. *I will NOT let Oliver get to me today.*

Ugh. Even thinking his name made me feel upset. So, I decided to start calling him "Olive Boy." It took a little bit of the power away from his name. Plus, it sounded kind of funny. I imagined his head as a giant green olive with a toothpick sticking out of it and instantly felt better. *You've got this, Siarra!*

For the most part, the class went off pretty well. We ran through the usual activities without incident. Then, towards the end of the class, Jill asked the students to form two lines of five, and Mia and I quickly moved into a group together.

But our excitement soon changed to dread when Jill explained the exercise. Each of us would race against our counterpart in the other group.

"I hate racing against other people," I muttered under my breath.

"Me too," Mia said.

I raised my hand. "Why can't we just race against ourselves?"

"That's a very good question, Siarra. And we should

always be striving to do our personal best. But since some of you have expressed an interest in speed skating and competition, I thought we'd give something different a try."

"Awesome," Oliver said, grinning. "This'll be fun."

When some of the other kids smiled and nodded their approval, Mia and I slumped our shoulders. We seemed to be the only two people not excited about this.

"Let's give it a try and see how it goes," Jill said.

I shrugged. "Okay." What was I supposed to do? If Jill thought it was a good idea, it couldn't be that bad, right?

Jill went over the rules, which were pretty straight-forward. She would raise her hand to indicate it was time to get ready, and when she dropped her hand, you had to try to get to the other side faster than your opponent.

I didn't care who I raced as long as it wasn't *him*. I looked over to see who I'd be up against. *Phew.* Thankfully, I'd be up against a different boy, and we'd be going last.

Jill skated to the opposite side of the rink and raised her hand, and as soon as she dropped it, the first two skaters pushed off. It was actually pretty exciting. I could see why some of the kids wanted to do it.

When the first racers finished, Jill gave them some

pointers. But before long, her hand went up again, indi-cating it was time for the next race.

The next two kids skated up to the red starting line, and Jill dropped her hand. This one wasn't even close. The taller girl was named Lucy. She was much faster and easily won the race.

Mia was up next. Jill's hand went down, and the skaters were off.

Everyone was rooting for their favorite, and I was rooting for Mia (of course). It was close, but Mia came out the winner.

"Woo-hoo!" I yelled. "Way to go, Mia!"

When I looked over at the next two contestants, I realized that Olive Boy had switched places. And would now be racing against me. He caught my eye and sneered.

I looked away, but it was too late. He was already inside my head. *You're never going to beat me*, Olive Boy's voice said. *You're too slow.*

No. I wasn't going to let him get to me. Not today. I was ready for this. I took three long, deep breaths to calm my nerves.

One.

Two.

Three.

"You've got this," I whispered to myself.

I imagined I was an Olympic speed skater. Even better, I imagined I was the fastest skater in the world.

I glanced over at Olive Boy again. He slid his finger across his throat to indicate that I was dead.

But I wasn't fazed by it at all. Instead, I laughed at him, which made him really mad. He gritted his teeth and made an angry face. Which made me laugh even more. Which made him *really, really* mad.

"You're slow and I'm fast!" he called over at me.

Inside my mind, I just kept repeating, *You've got this, Siarra!*

"You'll NEVER beat me!" he growled, but I ignored him and kept my eyes on Jill as she raised her arm.

Olive Boy was so mad now, he wasn't even paying attention. Maybe *I* was in *his* head.

When Jill's arm dropped, I pushed off as hard as I could, taking an early lead over my distracted opponent. My heart pounded. My legs pumped. I knew I was skating fast, because it felt like I was flying.

I'm in the lead. I'm actually going to win! I'm going to beat him!

The kids at the finish line screamed with excitement. The finish line was within reach. I was almost there!

I'm going to—

Something hit my left skate so hard that it pushed my foot right off the ice. And as I tried to regain my balance, something else—something much bigger—smashed into me from behind.

It must have happened in a millisecond, but it seemed like time stood still. My legs shot out from under me and I fell backward.

If this were a movie, this is where everything would go into slow motion. They'd show my body slowly flying into the air, and then they'd do a close up of my terrified face. My mouth would look ridiculous as I mouthed the word "Nooooooooo!"

WHAM!

I hit the ice. Hard.

And now I understood why they made us wear helmets. As my feet had flown up into the air, my head had rocked backward and smashed into the ice. Even with a brand-new helmet, my world was shaken. I wasn't knocked unconscious, but if this were a cartoon, there would've been little birdies flying around my head.

I lay flat on my back and stared up at the arena rafters.

"Are you two okay?"

My eyes refocused. Jill was leaning over me with a worried face. What happened? I literally didn't know what hit me. And why had Jill said, "Are you *two* okay?" What was she talking about?

"OLIVER!" Jill yelled. "Wait over there!"

Of course! It was HIM! The big ape couldn't stand losing. He knew I was going to win the race, so he must have knocked me down on purpose.

I struggled to get up, but I couldn't move. Oh no! Was I dead? Nope. In addition to knocking me down, Olive Boy had also knocked the wind out of me.

Mia crouched down next to me. "Can you breathe?"

"Don't try to get up, Siarra," Jill said. "Just take your time and try to breathe slowly."

If you've ever had the wind knocked out of you, you know what I felt like. But if you've never experienced it, let me try to explain.

Imagine someone put a machine down your throat that sucked all your guts out. Imagine every single muscle in your body squeezing your insides at the same time. Imagine what it would feel like if you could never breathe again.

To put it mildly, it really sucked! Thankfully it didn't last that long, and after a few minutes, I was able to sit up slowly.

I watched as Dad slipped his way toward me across the ice. Jill intercepted him and spoke to him briefly before skating over to Olive Boy. He was *definitely* getting in trouble this time.

"Siarra, are you okay?" Dad asked when he reached me.

I smiled weakly and nodded. "I'm okay, Dad."

"She got the wind knocked out of her," Mia said.

"Come on, honey." Dad and Mia each took an arm and helped me to my feet. The effort made me wheeze, which is the opposite of deep breathing. You try to inhale, but no matter how hard you try, it feels like you can't get enough air into your lungs.

Jill skated back over and joined us. "I'm so sorry, Siarra. Oliver's behavior was completely unacceptable! I'll be speaking with his parents." She took a few minutes and went through the concussion checklist with Dad and me. Basically, they check to make sure you don't need to go to the hospital. Thankfully, I passed. *Phew!*

"Siarra?" Dad asked again. "Are you *sure* you're okay?"

"I'm okay. Really." And as I said it, I realized that it was true. I *was* okay. In fact, I was more than okay. I was fast. If Olive Boy hadn't cheated, I would have won. And there were still three weeks until the end of class, so I was only going to get faster.

"Mia," Dad said. "Would you help Siarra over to the bench? I want to speak with Jill for a minute."

"Sure thing, Mr. Jones. No problem at all."

"That must have been so scary," Mia said as she

guided me over to the bench. "Are you sure you're all right?"

A smile grew from the corners of my mouth, then took over my entire face.

"Mia," I said. "I've never felt better."

8

THE LONG RIDE HOME

Jill made Olive Boy come over and apologize for tripping me, but it didn't seem very sincere. He kept his head down and stared at the ground. It was quick, but he did it, and then we all went our separate ways.

Dad and I had a long talk on the car ride home.

"It's not right," he said. "I don't think he should be allowed to come back at all."

"It's *okay*, Dad," I said for the hundredth time. "I can handle it. I'm not a baby anymore."

He sighed. "You're right, Siarra. You're strong and smart and you can handle a lot of things on your own."

I liked the sound of that, so I stayed quiet.

"But that type of behavior is unacceptable. I'm sorry that happened to you, Siarra, and I'm sure Jill's also sorry that something like this happened during her class."

I can't remember the last time I saw Dad look so serious. I don't know if I ever had.

"It's okay, Dad," I repeated.

"But it's *not* okay, Siarra. Kids being mean is one thing, but if Oliver, or anyone else, acts like a bully or makes you or your friends feel uncomfortable, promise me you'll tell an adult about it."

"Okay, but . . . it's hard sometimes."

"Yes, love, it *is* hard. Sometimes it's the hardest thing in the world to do. But that's why you need to do it. Sometimes being strong means sharing what's bothering you with others, especially adults. Think about the little kids that might not be as strong as you. We don't want to let bullies continue their bad behavior, right?"

I just nodded. I know Dad meant well, but I felt lousy.

"I'm really proud of you, Siarra. You've been working really hard on your skating. You're getting really good."

"Thanks Dad," I replied, feeling a little better.

He reached back and patted my leg. "And listen, you don't have to finish Jill's class if it makes you feel uncomfortable."

"What? What are you talking about? Of course I'm going to finish the class."

"I'm just saying it's okay if you don't want to."

I snorted. "I'm not going to let some jerk with a bad attitude ruin my fun."

"Are you sure?"

"I've never been more sure of anything in my life."

Dad winked. "All right then. It's settled."

"Good!"

But then I started to worry about what would happen to Jill. Would she still be able to teach classes? And if so, would she act differently around me? Would I still be able to take her summer class? Would she even want me?

"What did you say to Jill?" I demanded. "I don't want to get her in trouble."

"Jill isn't in any trouble. But, I spoke with her about the situation and we both agreed to keep a closer eye on Oliver. That's all."

"Good," I said, relieved.

"But remember, Siarra," he added. "Bullies don't always attack you head on. They can be sneaky too."

"I *know*, Dad." I rolled my eyes.

"Will you promise me you'll tell us if anything else happens?" he asked.

I nodded. I was tired and feeling kind of grumpy.

Who knew you could feel so many emotions in one day? It was kind of exhausting. Dad must have been exhausted too, because he stopped talking and turned up the radio. We didn't say anything the rest of the drive home.

When Dad and I got out of the car, he took my hand and squeezed it softly three times.

It was a secret code we'd come up with when I was little. Each squeeze stood for a single word: I. love. you.

I squeezed his hand four times in reply.

I. love. you. too.

"Siarra?"

"Yeah?"

Dad wrapped his arms around me and gave me a HUGE hug. "I love you," he whispered. "Don't ever forget that."

I smiled and squeezed him as tight as I could. "I love you too, Dad." I felt much better about everything.

We walked into the house together.

I guess, sometimes, maybe parents do understand.

9

PRACTICE, PRACTICE, PRACTICE

At dinner that night, Dad and I talked with Mom about the incident, but we didn't dwell on it. I was good. My parents were good. Everything was good. And with Oliver's apology, maybe the whole nasty episode was behind us. Hooray!

On Monday, Dad drove me to the rink so I could practice, and I spent over an hour working on the drills Jill had given us, especially the things I wasn't very good at. I was determined to pass this level so I could sign up for Jill's summer camp.

While I skated, I imagined there was a tiny little Jill sitting on my shoulder, encouraging me and guiding me through the exercises. And I did my best to follow her instructions exactly. Unlike a certain someone.

As I started my crossovers, Jill's reassuring voice

echoed in my mind. But skating around the red circle a few times in one direction then a few times in the other was *tiring*, especially after practicing so many other drills. After a few minutes, I got distracted and fell.

Don't get discouraged, Siarra, tiny Jill's voice said.

But I fell down!

I sat on the ice feeling sorry for myself, and before long, tiny Jill was joined by another tiny person.

Just give up and go home, tiny Olive Boy said.

Great. Now it was just like one of those old cartoons where two tiny people, one good and one bad, sit on opposite shoulders.

But even though imaginary tiny Olive Boy's voice was louder, I focused on tiny Jill's voice. *Remember, each time you fall and get back up, you're getting stronger.*

So I got up, giggling to myself as I imagined a tiny red-faced Olive Boy waving his fists at her from my other shoulder.

Don't get discouraged, tiny Jill whispered into my ear. Then she repeated something I'd heard her say in class. *Remember, step-by-step and you will succeed.* But the time had come to focus on my own voice. "You've got this," I said out loud, then continued practicing my crossovers.

After a few minutes, something clicked inside my mind *and* my body. I was doing proper crossovers! And not only one, but lots of them.

I'd heard people talk about being in "the zone" before, but I'd never experienced it myself. I was relaxed, but focused. One single move. There was nothing else. And, when I finished that move, I focused on the next single move. Again. Nothing else mattered.

One.

After.

Another.

Step.

By.

Step.

The more I relaxed but stayed focused, the better my crossovers became. And as one skate moved over the other, I realized what Jill had meant in class (and in my head) when she'd said, "Step-by-step and you will succeed." It was just another way of saying if you want to get good at something, you need to practice, practice, and then practice some more.

When I finished my crossovers, I decided to try hockey stops. Why not? I was in the zone, right?

Not exactly. I soon discovered that to get in the zone for hockey stops, I would need a lot more practice.

Proper hockey stops are hard to explain and even harder to do (I know this because I've heard many skating teachers try to explain them). Okay, here goes. To complete a hockey stop, you skate forward, lift your strong leg, rotate your hips, lean back, and turn your body to the side so that both skates are sideways. Then, you plant your back foot and dig your skates in until you stop. Sounds easy, right?

Wrong.

Here are three things to remember when you're trying to do a hockey stop:

Ice is hard.

Hockey stops are hard.

Falling on ice while trying to do a hockey stop hurts. A LOT.

I tried to do a hockey stop and fell on my side. *Ouch!* But I got up and tried again. And again. And again.

Then, I *didn't* fall. I sort of skidded. So I tried again. I skidded again. Again. And again.

When I finally skated off the ice, I felt pretty proud of myself. It was the best skating I had ever done. Yes, my hockey stops were still far from perfect, but I'd made some great progress. And I didn't need tiny Olive Boy's voice to tell me it was time to go—my butt did it for him. After all, a person can only fall so many times in one day.

10

AN ANGRY BULL!

Finally, it was time for Jill's class. I wasn't too nervous about seeing Oliver, since after the apology, I figured he and I were okay. Sure, we'd never become best friends, but I was willing to put the whole mess behind us.

Once we were on the ice, Jill explained that today, we'd continue working on our crossovers. Woo-hoo! I couldn't wait to show off all my hard work.

After a quick warm-up skate, we split into two groups and started practicing. Everyone did their best, but crossovers aren't easy. Doing them while standing is one thing, but trying to do them while skating around in a circle was another story altogether. Kids were falling down left and right. And when one kid would fall, then another kid would run into the fallen kid and topple over them. It was like watching a silly comedy show.

"Don't give up!" I said to one of the boys who'd fallen. He smiled gratefully at me as he got to his feet.

On one hand, I felt bad for the kids who were trying really hard but still weren't getting it. On the other hand, I felt pretty proud of myself. My skating had improved a lot in a short time, and I hadn't fallen down once.

Jill even came over and gave me some kudos. "Nice work, Siarra. I can tell you've been practicing."

"It's true," I replied. "Step-by-step—it really works."

"Keep it up, and soon you'll be doing backward crossovers too."

I imagined myself effortlessly gliding backward, arms extended, outside skate rhythmically crossing over. I could get used to this—feeling like Jill's star student.

I was having so much fun, I wished the class would never end. But with five minutes left, Jill called us over.

"Okay, for the last few minutes, we're going to play freeze tag," Jill said. "Who wants to be 'it?'"

Oliver's hand shot up faster than anyone else's.

"Anyone else?" Jill asked, looking around but no one else put up their hand. "No? All right," Jill said. "Oliver it is. On your mark. Get set. Go!" Skaters sped off in all directions.

I was tired from the workout, so I was planning to simply skate around and chat with Mia. But then I looked up and saw Oliver skating toward me at top speed, eyes narrowed and nostrils flared. He didn't even try tagging the kids who skated right in front of him—he just skated around. He had only one target. Me.

Okay! Maybe Oliver *hadn't* moved on. I skated away from Mia. No need to bring her—or any other innocent bystander—down with me.

Olive Boy (I reverted to calling him this in my head) was gaining on me. I skated as fast as I could, but there was only so much space at our end of the rink—we weren't supposed to go past the blue line—and I soon found myself trapped in a corner with Olive Boy coming in fast.

Then, I got an idea.

A WILD idea.

Olive Boy looked like an angry bull; he was acting like an angry bull. So I imagined a cartoon where an angry bull charged at a bullfighter.

I slowed down as I approached the corner. Olive Boy skated straight for me.

Wait for it.

Olive Boy skated closer.

Wait for it.

Olive Boy was almost on top of me.

NOW!

11

SUCKERED!

Unfortunately, my plan didn't go *exactly* as I'd imagined.

Sure, Olive Boy had smashed into the wall, but as he'd flown by, he'd stuck out his arm and tagged me. I was FROZEN. And Olive Boy was getting up.

"You're *slow*," he said with a smirk. "You're so slow, you're frozen."

Dad was right about bullies sometimes being more subtle. With his back to everyone else, Olive Boy skated right up to my face and whispered his threats. "And you're going to *stay* frozen for the rest of the game."

True to his word, Olive Boy tagged anyone that tried to come near me. But, believe it or not, I actually felt kind of sorry for him. He was trying to intimidate me, but it wasn't going to work. Not this time. I wasn't afraid of him anymore.

So I'm frozen for a few minutes. So what? Who cares?

Before long, the game finished and Jill called everyone over.

As I skated up to join the group, Olive Boy gloated to some of the other skaters. "Siarra was frozen for the whole game!"

"So what?" I replied. "You're going to stay stupid for the rest of your life!" Now *that's* what you call a burn. I expected his jaw to hit the ice, but it didn't.

"Oliver and Siarra!" Jill's voice called out from behind us. "That is enough!"

That's when I saw Olive Boy's face. Something was different . . . something was up. He looked right at me and smiled.

I'd been set up.

He suckered me in, and I fell for it. Hook, line, and sinker. I imagined myself looking like a giant lollipop. SU-C-K-E-R spells *sucker*, and that was exactly what I felt like.

"Oliver and Siarra, please stay after class," Jill said. "You can wait for me on the away bench. But you are NOT to speak to one another."

We skated over to the bench in silence. It felt like were being sent to the penalty box.

As all the other kids skated out of the rink, I saw Dad

heading toward me. I hated getting into trouble. It sucked!

Olive Boy, on the other hand, must be used to getting into trouble by now.

When Jill and my dad arrived, I tried to explain what happened. "Olive— I mean *Oliver* tricked me! He skated right at me, without even tagging anyone else. Then he wouldn't let anyone else unfreeze me. Then . . ." Realizing how silly the whole thing sounded, I swallowed the rest of my words.

Olive Boy didn't say anything. Not a word. He slumped his shoulders and hung his head. He played the victim role really well.

Jill crossed her arms. "I need both of you to listen carefully. I know you've had your differences, but I need this behavior to stop. Right now. I won't have this type of bad sportsmanship in my class."

I apologized to Olive Boy for calling him stupid. He apologized to me for not letting anyone else get close enough to unfreeze me.

Then Jill gave us an ultimatum. "If either of you want to take any classes with me in the future, I need you to promise me that you'll behave better. Do you promise to try and get along?"

We both nodded.

"Okay, then," she said. "I'll see you both next week."

I skated off the ice *a lot* less excited than when I first arrived. Dad told me not to take it too hard, but I was pretty mad at myself.

Even though Olive Boy tricked me, it was still my own fault I got in trouble. I shouldn't have said what I said. I knew better than that.

Still, how could people not see what a bully Olive Boy was?

I loved my parents, but my stomach ached at the thought of going over everything again with them. I wanted to barf. "You should know better. Blah, blah, blah. Take the high road. Blah, blah, blah. We're very disappointed. Blah, blah, blah." Sometimes parents just didn't get it.

The ride home in the car with Dad was . . . weird. He kept trying to talk with me about things, but I didn't feel like it.

I already knew what Dad would say anyway. "You shouldn't let people get under your skin." Then he'd add, "You shouldn't let other people make you so mad." Then, he'd finish up with his two favorite lines. "If you get angry, you automatically lose. You can't control other people, but you can control how you react to them." Just thinking about it was getting me upset. I took my three breaths.

One.

Two.

Three.

Then I realized that these conversations with my parents were just in my head, and I let out a big sigh of relief.

Sometimes, my brain was weird. Sometimes I got more upset by the stories I made up than my real-life problems. Sometimes, if I thought too much about something, it made it worse than it actually was.

Dad gave up and turned up the radio.

I peered out the window and daydreamed that I was a bird flying high above the car. It was weird, but looking at my situation from way up there, things down here didn't seem that bad.

When we pulled into the driveway, Dad looked over his shoulder at me sitting in the back seat.

"Don't worry, Siarra," he said softly. "Jill knows you've been working really hard. You're going to do great."

"Thanks Dad."

"And now that you know how tricky Oliver can be, you won't be fooled into losing your temper again." He smiled and winked at me.

Wow. Maybe sometimes parents actually *do* get it.

"Because if you lose your temper," he added, "you've already lost."

Okay. And sometimes they really don't.

OPEN EYES

Have you ever noticed that when you learn a new word, you start to hear it all the time?

Or, when you're on a long car trip and you play punch buggy, suddenly you start seeing VW Bugs everywhere? (Our family has played punch buggy since I was little, only we never punch each other, we just count how many cars we can see. The game goes on forever and no one ever really wins.)

It's like, even though you never noticed something before, now that you've seen that thing, you can't stop seeing it. You notice it everywhere.

Well, now that I'd gotten up close and personal with a real-life bully, I started to see bullying (or at the very least, mean behavior) happening all over the place. And it wasn't like Oliver was the first person to ever be mean to me. But for whatever reason, the experience opened my eyes.

At lunch one day, I was walking with Mia and saw an older boy named Jayden knock Alphie's binder out of his arms. Papers fell out of the binder and blew all over the schoolyard.

It dawned on me that this wasn't the first time I'd seen this happen. In fact, when I thought about it, I realized that I'd seen Jayden do this many times before. I even remembered hearing him brag about doing it to others. That wasn't just being mean—that was bullying.

Until now, I'd never really noticed or cared about it. Mia and I would have just kept walking, the same way Jayden just kept walking.

Not today!

I ran over and helped Alphie pick up his stuff, while Mia grabbed some papers that had flown farther away and brought them over to us.

"Thanks a lot," Alphie said as he put everything back into his binder.

"No problem. Take it easy, Alphie."

Mia and I continued on.

We'd learned about bullying in school, of course. The teachers and principal talked about it a lot. There was even a National Stop Bullying Day. It was sometimes called Pink Shirt Day, because everyone was supposed to wear a pink shirt to school, and was supposed to bring more attention to bullying. But honestly, I'd never really understood what it meant. Until now.

Trust me, kids who were being bullied didn't need a pink shirt to remind them about it. It sucked. I always knew that, but now I REALLY knew it.

Every student at Central Elementary was taught the difference between being mean and being an actual bully. Lots of kids were randomly mean. But that didn't make it okay to call them "bullies." We'd learned that to be a real bully, a proper bully, you had to meet certain criteria.

Last year, all the students in our class had memorized the actual definition. We were even quizzed on it.

"Mia, do you remember the definition of bullying?" I asked.

Mia nodded, and we said it out loud together. *"Bullying is intentional, hurtful, and aggressive behavior that makes others feel uncomfortable, scared, or upset."*

Bullying wasn't just kids being mean. Or immature. And it wasn't just people disagreeing. It was much more than that. Officially, bullying had to include the following three things: hostile intent, imbalance of power, and repetition over a period of time. A bully had to act intentionally, have the power position, and repeat the action over time.

A few minutes later, Mia and I saw a boy throw a ball at another boy who was reading a book. We looked at each other.

"Bullying?" Mia asked.

"It's definitely mean," I replied. "If he does it every day it's definitely bullying."

Don't get me wrong. We saw lots of kids being nice: sharing lunches, playing games, exchanging notes. But it wasn't hard to find examples of kids being mean. And it wasn't just boys either.

A group of sixth-grade girls exited the school through the front doors.

As I said, to be a real bully, a proper bully, you have to follow certain rules. And there's one group of older girls who LOVE rules. They love making them and they love enforcing them. Emily, the leader of the group is tall and pretty and kind of scary. Everyone knows her, but lots of kids avoid her (and her mean group of friends), including Mia and me.

Emily was walking ahead, with her pack of mean friends trailing closely behind her like puppies. Unfortunately, these puppies were anything but cute. They were vicious. We stopped immediately to avoid them seeing us.

Emily walked down the front steps and called out to a girl sitting alone on the bottom step. "Nice outfit, Surita," she said sweetly. "Once again, you've simply outdone yourself. What do you call that outfit . . . *hand-me-down fabulous?*"

Surita's face sank.

"Hand-me-down fabulous," the other girls repeated, laughing loudly as they all walked past Surita.

"Totally!" one of the mean girls said. "I love it."

Judging by the tone Emily and the other girls used, I could tell this wasn't the first time they'd been mean to Surita.

For a second, it looked like Surita might say something, but she didn't. The mean girls didn't even stop.

Mia looked at me again, "Bullying?"

"Yeah," I said. "I think so."

"Come on." Mia waved at Surita. "Let's go say hi."

This was why Mia was my best friend. She was kind. Thoughtful. AWESOME.

We walked over. "Hey, Surita," Mia said, smiling. "Want to join us for lunch?"

"I'm good," Surita said, sounding a little defeated. "But, thanks anyway."

Mia and I looked at each other and shrugged. We didn't want to push it, and we didn't really know what else to do.

"Well, if you change your mind," I offered, "we'll be over by the big cypress tree." Surita nodded, then went back to reading her book.

Mia and I sat down in our usual spot and looked around the schoolyard. Kids were playing and having fun, which made us feel a *little* better. Most kids weren't bullies. But it was still discouraging that we didn't even have to look very hard to find examples of bullying at our school.

Mia sighed. "Maybe it's a full moon?"

"More like a BULL moon!" I replied. We both cracked up, and *thank goodness.*

Thinking about all the injustice was exhausting. And the worst thing? None of the bullies we saw ever got in trouble.

13

A HERO APPEARS

The next day, Mia and I made our way up to the third floor of Central Elementary. After depositing our personal items in the coatroom, we took our seats.

All of the desks in Mr. Carter's fifth-grade classroom were arranged in sets of four. Our group included three girls—me, Mia, and Rene—and one boy named Jason. Jason was not happy about this arrangement at all. He constantly complained about his seat.

Of all the kids in our class, Jason was the biggest troublemaker. He got sent to the principal's office at least once a week. In fact, the reason Jason had joined our group was because Mr. Carter needed to separate him from his friends, Rohan and Mark.

I imagine there's someone like Jason in every class. Sometimes it's a boy. Sometimes it's a girl. I don't know why, but there are always people who don't care if they get into trouble. It's almost like they take pride in it.

Mia and I were just the opposite. We hated getting into trouble. The worst thing that ever happened to us was when Mr. Carter threatened to separate us for goofing around in math class. The fear of being separated was all it took—we were on our best behavior from that moment on. We even stopped passing notes, and trust me, that is NOT an easy thing to do. Especially for best friends.

When the lunch bell rang, all the kids rushed into the coatroom to grab their stuff. It was always a bit of a madhouse, with kids pushing and shoving. Kind of like the skating rink when everyone was fighting for a spot to sit down.

Our group of four was the farthest away from the coatroom, so we were usually the last ones to get our lunches. Today, Mia was faster than the rest of us. She grabbed her coat and lunch, then ran past me. "See you outside, usual spot."

Jason entered the coatroom next. "Out of my way, shrimp," he said, pushing Rene, who stood near her own cubby.

"Careful," Rene said softly as Jason grabbed his stuff.

"I barely touched you," Jason snapped. "Don't be such a baby."

Rene turned red and stared down at her feet. "I'm not a baby."

"Oh, yeah?" Jason lifted his lunchbox above his head, like he was going to bring it down on top of hers.

Suddenly, someone rushed past me. It was Taylor, one of the tallest girls in our grade. She wasn't in our class, but she must have been talking with Mr. Carter. He was also the coach of both the girls and the boys basketball teams.

"JASON!" Taylor yelled, so loud the whole school probably heard. "Stop it! Put that down, right now!" Getting in between them, she put her hands up in front of Rene protectively.

Taylor was totally fearless, and Jason could tell she meant business. He lowered his lunchbox. "What? I was just joking." He tried to leave, but Taylor blocked his way.

"Where do you think you're going?" she said, then turned to Rene. "Are you okay?"

Rene nodded. "I'm fine."

I didn't know what to do, so I just stood there, frozen.

Jason stood there too. "I didn't do anything," he whined. "Come on, Taylor. Move out of the way."

"We don't have to put up with this!" Taylor said, then yelled, "MR. CARTER!"

Mr. Carter entered the coatroom. "Is everything okay in here? What's going on?"

"Nothing," Jason said, trying to play it cool. "It's not a big deal."

Rene looked a bit shaken up by the whole thing. "It's okay. I'm fine." Her shoulders were hunched over like she was trying to make herself smaller. And that was saying a lot, because Rene was already one of the smallest kids in our class.

Taylor scowled. "It's not fine. Jason threatened to hit her."

"What? Is that true, Rene?"

"It's okay, Mr. Carter." Rene stared at the floor. "Can we just go for lunch?"

"Sorry. Not until we get to the bottom of this." He motioned for us to leave the coatroom and then had us line up in front of his desk. "Now, Rene. Can you tell me exactly what happened?"

It wasn't really fair for Mr. Carter to ask Rene to explain things, especially with Jason standing right next to her. What if Jason told everyone she was a snitch?

Taylor must have felt the same way because she jumped in. "Jason threatened to hit Rene with his lunch-box. He held it over his head like *this*." She mimicked Jason's earlier actions.

"It was just a joke! I wasn't going to really hit her."

"Jason," Mr. Carter said. "Is that the kind of behavior we should expect from you?"

Jason looked down at the floor. "No."

"I didn't think so. Now, please go outside and wait for me in the hallway."

Jason slunked out of the classroom. "Can't anyone take a joke?" he muttered.

"That's enough, Jason," Mr. Carter said calmly. "Don't make this worse for yourself."

"You threatened Rene!" Taylor called after him. "We saw you!" She looked at me for support. "Right?"

I just nodded, really, really fast. Now I was involved too, whether I liked it or not.

"Thank you, Taylor," Mr. Carter said, then looked at Rene. "I'm sorry that happened to you. Are you sure you're all right?"

"Yeah. I'm okay."

"Well, Jason and I are going to have a chat with the principal. You girls go and enjoy the rest of your lunch."

Mr. Carter walked over to the door and opened it for us. Jason was sitting outside in the hallway with his head in his hands, but jumped to his feet when he saw us leaving the classroom. Taylor glared at him, but he kept his head down and avoided her eyes.

Mr. Carter and Jason headed toward the principal's

office, and we walked in the opposite direction toward the nearest exit.

"Jason is just trying to act tough," Taylor said, putting her arm around Rene's shoulder.

"Let's just forget about it," Rene said. "But thanks for stepping in, Taylor."

"Yeah, Taylor, you were amazing," I blurted out as we walked downstairs. "Weren't you scared?" I was acting like a total fangirl, but I didn't care. She was amazing.

"Honestly? I was so mad, I didn't even have time to think about it."

"Well, I'm glad you were there," Rene said.

"We're friends," Taylor replied. "We've got to look out for each other, right?"

Rene nodded, and I wished Taylor was my friend too. I made a mental note to say hi to her every time I saw her from now on.

As soon as we got outside the school, I ran to the cypress tree and told Mia everything that had happened.

"I'm glad someone finally stood up to Jason," she said. "His stupid jokes are not funny—at all!"

I nodded. "I feel kind of bad that I didn't do more."

"Don't worry about it, Siarra. Sometimes you want to do something, but you just can't. It happens to all of us. And you're braver than most."

"Do you really think so?"

"I *know* so."

Mia always knew how to make me feel better. Sometimes it was just a look, but other times she said exactly the right thing at exactly the right time.

We played until the end-of-lunch bell rang, and when we got back to our classroom, Mr. Carter had a long talk with the whole class about inappropriate physical behavior. Though he never mentioned Jason by name.

I found out a few days later that Jason and his parents were asked to speak with the school counselor. Plus, he was going to have to attend something called restorative justice classes.

Finally, I thought. *A bully got in trouble.*

14

DIE OF FRIGHT?

Today was the big day—the final class of Level Five skating—the day that would determine if I would pass and be allowed to sign up for Jill's skating camp. All week it felt as if it would never arrive, but it was finally here.

Last week's class had been all practice for the final, and thankfully, Oliver and I had stayed far away from each other. I'd put in another extra practice session after that, so I felt as prepared as I could be.

When I skated onto the ice, I could feel the tension in the air. Oliver was skating back and forth between the blue line and the red line. He never stopped. Not even for a minute. It was like he was a shark that needed to keep moving in order to stay alive.

I glided up to Mia. "How are you doing?"

"I'm not going to pass," she said matter-of-factly, then shrugged.

I wanted to encourage her the same way she always encouraged me. "You never know. You've been working hard."

"I still can't do proper crossovers. And I *definitely* can't do a hockey stop."

Before I could say anything else, Jill skated over to the group, accompanied by a teenager.

"Okay, everyone," she announced. "As you all know, today is our last class. This is Amita. She's training to become an instructor and is going to be helping me with the final tests."

Amita grinned and waved. "This is going to be fun, right?"

Fun? No. Terrifying? Yes. Unlike most other teenagers I've met, Amita seemed *very* enthusiastic. Maybe a little *over*enthusiastic?

"Is everyone ready for an exciting day of skating?" she said, clapping her hands together. "This is going to be amazing!"

We all stared at her blankly.

Thankfully, Jill jumped in. "For the first half of the class, Amita and I will split up and spend time with each of you. Then we'll do the testing in the second half."

As we practiced, it was easy to see that everyone's skating had improved. A few kids were still having trouble with their crossovers, though, and most of the students still sucked at hockey stops. I did okay with them. Not great, but better than most. And definitely better than when I first started the class.

Jill blew her whistle. Practice time was over, and final testing was about to begin.

"We've set up two identical courses," she said, "and you'll be given marks as you work your way through each section. In order to pass Level Five, you have to make it through the entire course."

I took a deep breath and glanced over at the courses. The rink seemed a lot larger than usual. I don't know why everything looked *bigger*, but it did.

"It's not about who's the fastest," Jill said. "Speed does count, but today is mostly about showing me your skills and your control. You need to show me that you can stay focused and complete each exercise. Especially in a competitive environment."

Jill explained how the test would work: Small orange cones had been placed along the full length of the rink, and for the first part you needed to glide on one foot toward the cone, go around it, switch legs and do the same to the next cone, and so on, until you were all the way across the ice.

The second part of the test was basically the same, only you had to do it going backward.

The third part of the test was crossovers around the red face-off circle. Each skater pushed off four times with their outside skate, then turned around and did the same thing going the opposite way with the opposite leg.

The fourth and final part of the test was about speed and stopping. Each student would skate the full length of the rink and finish with a hockey stop at the far end.

The more she talked, the more nervous I became. *Great.* I was already freaking out and we hadn't even started yet.

"Step-by-step and you will succeed," I whispered to myself.

Jill held up a baseball cap so everyone could see it. "I've put all your names in this hat. You will be tested, two by two, in the order that I pull your names out."

Amita pulled out each name and Jill called them out.

One. Two. Three. Mia's name was called out. *Four.*

"And take note, everyone," Jill added. "Students who watch and cheer on the other students will get bonus points for showing a positive attitude." She called out the next set of names.

Five. Six. Seven. Eight.

My name still wasn't called, and the waiting was making me even more nervous. Then I realized there were only two names left, mine and . . . *Oh no!*

Maybe I misheard. Maybe Jill would call out someone else's name. There was no way I could have luck *this* bad. If this were in a movie, people wouldn't believe it.

Jill called out Oliver's name. *Nine.*

My stomach sank.

"There's only one name left in here," Jill said, looking at me. "I'm guessing it's yours."

She pulled out the final piece of paper and read the name on it. "Siarra."

I felt sick to my stomach. I wasn't really afraid of Oliver . . . right now I felt afraid of *everything*. But it didn't make any sense. Where did all my confidence go? A few minutes ago, I was feeling pretty good. Now, I wanted to go home and hide under my cozy blanket.

"Oliver and Siarra," Jill said, snapping me back to reality. "I know you two will be true to your word and handle this like good sports. Right?"

I could hardly breathe, but I nodded and said, "Yes."

Oliver did the same.

15

BATTLE OF THE SKATES

Amita led everyone over to the home hockey players' bench and told us wait until our names were called. Then, after reminding us to cheer on our classmates, she skated over to join Jill at the starting lines.

The two instructors would watch their respective skater as they made their way through the course, Jill grading one student and Amita grading the other.

Jill called the first two students over—a boy named Wes and Lucy, the tall girl—and we wished them good luck. They took their positions at the blue line.

Wes was a pretty good skater, but Lucy was excellent, one of the best in our class.

Jill blew her whistle—the race was on! (I know Jill said it wasn't supposed to be a race, but it sure felt like one.)

Both skaters completed the first and second sections with no problems at all, and they were neck and neck. Mia and I cheered them both from the sidelines, and most of the other kids joined in. Everyone except for you-know-who, of course. Parents and friends scattered throughout the stands also joined in the cheering.

In the third section, Wes was going strong, but Lucy messed up one of her crossovers and fell.

"Oh!" A loud gasp came from someone in our cheering section.

Jill quickly skated over and encouraged Lucy to keep going, and when she got back up, everyone cheered. The cheering must have made her feel better because she finished the third section without any more trouble and finished the fourth section with a spectacular hockey stop.

Jill whispered something to Lucy that made her smile, then glided over to Wes (and Amita) and gave him a pat on the shoulder. And when the two kids skated to the away players' bench, we all cheered and gave them fist bumps as they passed by.

Next, Jill called over Mia and the girl she'd be skating with.

"Good luck, Mia," I said. "You're going to do great."

"Thanks," she replied, then hopped onto the ice.

Once Mia and the other girl were at the starting line, Jill blew her whistle and they took off. They were evenly matched in skill level, and although neither of them broke any speed records, they both finished the first two sections without any trouble. Unfortunately, neither of them could get their crossovers right. No one fell down, but neither of them completed the section properly.

In the final section, the other girl pulled way ahead. Mia was not feeling confident and it showed.

"Go Mia!" I called out to her. "You can do it!"

The rest of the crowd joined me in cheering her on, and she skated through section four without any problems. But when she made it to the finish line, she didn't even try to do a hockey stop.

I waved to her, but she didn't notice me until she and her partner skated over to join the others on the away bench.

"You were awesome, Mia!" I said as she went by.

She gave me a little smile.

The next two kids were almost perfect on every section, and even their crossovers were awesome. When they got to the last section, they pulled out all the stops and skated as fast as they could, so fast I thought they would smash through the boards. But at the last second, they both did amazing hockey stops that shot waves of shaved ice high into the air. Everyone cheered so loud it sounded like a professional sporting event.

The next pair was slow but steady. They made it through the whole course without any major problems.

I was having a great time cheering everyone on, but before I knew it, my joy and excitement turned to dread. Oliver and I were next. We'd avoided looking at each other the whole class—he'd sat at the far end of the bench, and I'd sat at the other end, near the door—but the time to face him had arrived.

My hands were all sweaty, and it felt like my heart was beating a million miles a minute. I needed to get things back under control. Deep breaths.

One.

Two.

Three.

Jill called out our names.

"Good luck, Oliver," I said as I stepped onto the ice.

He glared at me. "You're so slow, you'll need all the luck you can get."

I didn't react, just whispered, "You've got this, Siarra," and pushed off toward the starting line.

Oliver jumped onto the ice and pretended to cough as he skated past me, but added the word "loser" at the end.

You're slow! I'm fast! tiny Oliver's voice yelled inside

my head. But I reminded myself that this wasn't a race, that there was nothing to be afraid of. All I had to do was stay focused and remember my practice.

Step-by-step and you will succeed.

A calmness came over me as I reached the starting line. I looked down at my panda socks and smiled, then glanced over at Oliver.

He stuck his tongue out at me.

I decided to keep my eyes straight ahead, determined to stay focused. "You've got this," I repeated to myself. I could feel Oliver's eyes watching me, but I ignored him. I wasn't going to let him get to me. Not today.

Jill blew her whistle and I pushed off as hard as I could. I could feel my muscles flexing, and I could hear people in the crowd, especially Dad, cheering me on. I made it through section one and two without any trouble.

Oliver was a fast skater, but with all of my extra practicing, I was fast too. By the time we reached the crossover section, we were neck and neck.

I wanted to do my crossovers exactly as I did them during my practices, so I slowed down and took my time. It felt good. Actually, it felt great. I was in the same zone I'd found during practice.

But halfway through the section, I looked over and

saw Oliver pull ahead of me. Bad move. I should have known better. I *did* know better.

I felt myself getting upset, but I couldn't help it. I just wanted to beat him! I'd worked so hard. I'd pract—

Oh no!

My skate caught an edge. I almost fell.

Almost.

But my practice saved me. After all that hard work, it would be foolish to let him get the best of me. And this was about me, not him. I took a deep breath, regained my focus, and went back to doing proper crossovers.

A voice screamed out and the crowd gasped in unison.

I looked up to see Oliver sliding toward me across the ice—he must have tripped doing one of his crossovers—and come to a stop a few feet from me.

"Are you okay?" I asked, offering him my hand.

But Oliver got up on his own and pushed me aside. "Get out of my way, loser!"

Time seemed to slow down—just like in the movies —and I felt a surge of energy course through my body. (If this *were* a movie, exciting music would be playing as the hero discovers their superhuman powers.)

Before I could even think about it, I pushed off as hard as I could. Oliver was ahead of me by at least three or four strides, but no matter. I crouched down and swung my arms like they do in speed skating, trying to get as much extra momentum as I could.

He skated fast.

I skated faster.

And in only a few seconds, I was less than half a stride behind him. The crowd cheered us on, and I felt a thrill surge through me. I was gaining on him!

Oliver noticed me out of the corner of his eye and skated faster.

But so did I.

We were skating neck and neck now, like two lightning bolts whizzing across the ice toward the boards. And with only a few feet left, something almost magical happened.

I actually passed him!

But then I had a moment of panic. Yes, I'd practiced my hockey stops, but they weren't always very strong. I didn't know if I'd be able to do it. Especially at this speed.

Oh, well! If I died smashing into the boards, it was worth it.

At the very last second, I pushed my knees together and turned my hips as forcefully as I could. My blades scraped hard against the ice and sprayed some ice shavings into the air.

SWOOSH!

I did it! My best hockey stop ever!

SMASH!

Oliver had skated right into the boards.

Hard.

All the cheering stopped, and Jill and Amita rushed over to make sure he was okay. Fortunately, he was. A bit stunned, but otherwise fine. When he got up, the crowd burst into applause.

I skated over to Mia and the other kids, who were all hooting and hollering. Everyone congratulated me. I felt so good, I thought I was going to cry.

"You were amazing!" Mia screamed. She pulled me close into a giant bear hug. "A-MAAY-ZING!"

Amita skated over to the bench and congratulated us all on a job well done, then winked at me. "Great job, Siarra."

Jill was still with Oliver at the end of the rink and looked to be having a serious talk with him. I don't know what she said, but he shook his head angrily, then skated right past everyone and headed straight for the exit.

I couldn't be sure, but it looked like he was crying.

Jill skated over and congratulated everyone. I waited patiently as she handed out the skating report cards, offering each skater a few final words of encouragement.

Mia was one of the first to get hers, and when she read it, she looked at me and shook her head.

I gave her a big hug. "Sorry, Mia. You'll get it next time for sure."

"Thanks, Siarra. I knew I didn't pass this one. I'll call you later." She skated over to join her mother off the ice.

You could tell who would be advancing and who wouldn't by the looks on their faces. No one looked surprised, though. I guess everyone had a pretty good idea whether they passed or not. But I wasn't sure. I *thought* I did pretty well, but I messed up my crossovers in that one section, and the final race was a bit of a blur . . .

"Congratulations, Siarra!" Jill held out my skating report card. "Your skating has improved, and you showed an excellent attitude. I'd be pleased to invite you to my skating camp. Step-by-step—"

But before she could even finish the sentence, I threw my arms around her and hugged her with all my might. I may have even lifted her off the ground.

Oliver wasn't the only one who left the rink crying that day. By the time I reached Dad, I was a blubbering mess.

"I'm so proud of you," he said. "You were absolutely fantastic!" He beamed from ear to ear, which only made me cry even more.

It's weird, isn't it? You cry when you're sad and you cry when you're happy.

I definitely prefer the happy kind of crying.

16

THE CONFRONTATION

When Dad and I sat down in the change area, Oliver was just finishing taking off his skates. An older boy—about sixteen or seventeen—was with him. Maybe his brother?

As Oliver picked up his equipment to leave, the older boy smacked him across the head. "Hurry up! You're so slow." He smacked Oliver again, then shoved him from behind. I got the feeling that Oliver got smacked a lot.

My face got hot. No wonder Oliver behaved the way he did! I'm not sure what came over me—maybe it was adrenaline left over from the class, or maybe I was upset at seeing someone else being bullied—but I handed Dad my helmet and told him to hold my spot, then ran over to the two boys.

I stopped right in front of the older one. Even in my skates, I was still shorter than him. He was holding Oliver by his jacket.

"Stop that RIGHT NOW!" I yelled loud enough for everyone to hear. "That is NOT okay!"

"What are you talking about?" the older boy said. He tried to walk around me, pulling Oliver with him.

I moved and blocked his path. "Stop bullying him! Oliver, you don't have to put up with this!"

The older boy sneered. "Get out of my way, *psycho*."

I held my ground.

"Fine," he said. "I'm out of here." He released Oliver and walked around me toward the stairs. "Meet me at the car, loser," he yelled back to Oliver.

I tried to catch Oliver's eye, but he put his head down and walked around me too.

"Oliver!"

He looked back at me with tears in his eyes. "What?"

"You don't have to put up with that kind of behavior."

"Yeah, right."

Dad joined us. "Is everything okay here?"

"I don't know," I replied, still looking at Oliver. "Is everything okay, Oliver? Was that your brother?"

"I gotta go." He headed toward the stairs.

"Hey!" I called out. "He's wrong, you know!"

He looked back at me, confused.

I was sad and confused too. "He's wrong," I said, tears running down my face. "He's WRONG!"

Oliver turned and ran up the stairs.

I could feel everyone staring at me. Dad put a hand on my shoulder, then pulled me in for a hug. A surge of emotions built up inside me. I felt like I was going to explode. I took in a long, deep breath and slowly released it.

"That was very brave of you, Siarra," he said.

I shook my head. "I couldn't help myself."

"Oliver might not have been able to say it, but I'm sure he appreciated what you did."

"I just felt like someone needed to stand up for him."

"Sometimes, that's all it takes."

We went back to the bench, and I took off my skates. And in a few short minutes, we were walking to the car.

"SIARRA!"

I looked over and saw Oliver waving at me frantically from a car window.

He smiled, then yelled to me as the car sped away, "You're not SLOW, you're FAST! YOU'RE FAST!"

Dad and I looked at each other, surprised, then burst out laughing. Well, what do you know, maybe I *had* made a difference!

"So, Speedy," Dad said when we reached the car. "How about some ice cream to celebrate?"

"Sounds good, Dad."

I threw my bag in the trunk and hopped in the car. And as we drove out of the parking lot, I rolled down my window, stuck my head out, and screamed at the top of my lungs. "My name is Siarra Jones! I'm a Level Six, and I LOVE SKATING!"

THE END

THANK YOU

Thank you for reading *Siarra Jones Skating Into Trouble,* book 1 in my Step-by-Step series. I hope you enjoyed the story as much as I enjoyed writing it. If you did, please consider leaving a review to help others discover my writing. It really makes a difference.

Amazon review:
www.amazon.com/dp/B08IDRFF2S

Goodreads review:
www.goodreads.com/book/show/48847734-siarra-jones-skating-into-trouble

See the next page to read the first chapter of the next book in the Step-by-Step series,

Jake Murphy and the Karate Choke.

I hope you'll enjoy this one too.

Sincerely,
Paul Breau

JAKE MURPHY AND THE KARATE CHOKE

I

Choke and Die of Embarrassment

I couldn't breathe. When I stood up from my desk, my legs were heavy and my head felt light. I looked ahead to the front of the classroom and walked up the aisle. Everything moved slowly, like I was walking through water.

Was that my heartbeat? Why was it going so fast? Should it be taking this long to get to the front of the class?

Oh no! I think I have to pee!

I finally made it to the teacher's desk and slowly

turned to face the class—then froze completely, unable to speak. I felt hot, too hot. Sticky hot.

Say something!

Why was I just standing there? Why was I sweating so much? Why was I so *gross*?

I couldn't think straight. Couldn't breathe. Couldn't move.

What's happening? Something's wrong! I'm going to die . . . I am dying!

If you've ever heard the phrase "deer in the headlights," that was me. My name is Jake Murphy, and up until this moment, I was considered the smartest kid in Ms. Hardish's fifth grade class. That, however, was about to change. I was about to get run over by a giant truck called Anxiety.

I'd had panic attacks before, but never like this. And I'd never had trouble speaking in front of the class. In fact, I usually got into trouble for talking *too* much. So, none of this made any sense.

Ms. Hardish's sweet voice called out, "Jake, we're ready for you. You can start any time."

I'd studied. I knew this stuff. *Come on, man, you're ready!*

But I wasn't ready. I was anything *but* ready. And it didn't matter what I said to myself, I was stuck. Frozen.

"Choke!"

I recognized that sour voice immediately. It came from the meanest kid in my class, my archnemesis, "Mean Dean."

And he was right. I *was* choking. Badly. I was choking like no one had ever choked before. Great! I was going to be the first kid to choke and die of embarrassment.

Choke. That's the word people use when you were supposed to be able to do something, but when the time came to do it, you couldn't. As if I didn't have enough problems trying to survive fifth grade, now I couldn't talk or move. I was petrified!

I'd learned the word *petrified* when my family drove to North Dakota last summer. It was when a living tree turned into a rock, a real thing from the dinosaur age. The word's also used to describe someone who's really, really scared. When someone's so frightened they can't even move.

So not only was I choking, I was officially petrified.

Was this what comedians meant when they talked about "dying on stage"?

Well, I was no comedian, and this was not funny. I'd practiced my report at home all week. I knew it backward and forward. I'd memorized every word, every paragraph, every dramatic pause. I had even come up with some jokes.

But when my turn came, I forgot everything.

Every.

Single.

Thing.

I couldn't remember a word. Not one sentence, not one silly little joke. I couldn't even remember what I was supposed to talk about.

I looked around the class at all the blank faces staring back at me. My eyes got watery. It was like I was sinking in quicksand and was looking for something, *anything*, to stop me from going under.

Don't cry. Don't cry. Don't—

"Jake," Ms. Hardish said gently, looking down at her list. "You were going to tell us about fossils? You can start anytime now . . ."

Nothing. Even with Ms. Hardish's reminder, I had nothing. Nada. Zilch. Zero. And that was exactly what I was going to get on this assignment, zero. Because *I* was a zero. A zero who just stood there like a zombie. Then again, at least zombies could grunt and say "brains." I couldn't even do that!

Mean Dean mimicked the sound of radio static. "Earth to Jake," he said. "Come in, Jake."

Ugh! I hated him so much! Why couldn't he just leave me alone?

Dean was the type of kid that laughed when

someone fell and hurt themselves. Dean was the type of kid that would take your cap and throw it in a tree for no reason. The type of kid that came up with mean nicknames for everyone. Yep, you guessed it. Dean and I went all the way back to kindergarten.

"That's enough!" Ms. Hardish gave Dean a stern look, then turned back to me with an encouraging smile. "Take your time, Jake."

As I stood there, trying to unfreeze, Dean coughed "choke" under his breath. Then his little henchmen, Lenny and Shawn, joined him and they all started coughing the word. Soon it felt like the whole class was doing it.

"Choke, choke, choke," they quietly chanted.

But Ms. Hardish came to my rescue. "ENOUGH! The next person who speaks out will be sent to the principal's office."

The whole class went silent. Unfortunately, I remained silent as well.

Silent in English.

Silencio in Spanish.

Silencieux in French.

You can see why I was considered the smart kid in class. The other kids called me "the Brain" behind my back (and sometimes right to my face). I loved learning about new cultures and new languages. I loved words—words were my specialty. Not today.

Tears welled up in my eyes again. This was not good. Freezing in front of the whole class was bad enough, but crying? I would never live it down! Funny, this thought did *not* make me feel any better. Usually, my mind was my safe space. My thoughts were like good friends. Loyal, reliable, helpful, like my best friend, Matt.

Why was I such a jerk? Matt had wanted to do the presentation with me. But *no*, I had to be the smart guy, had to do the presentation all by myself. *Nice job!*

My brain seemed determined to make a bad situation worse. I wiped my eyes. I was able to move again, but my hands were shaking. *Thanks for nothing, brain.*

Wait. Did I hear something? I recognized that name . . .

"Jake?" Ms. Hardish called out my name again.

I didn't respond.

"Jake?"

I still didn't respond. I was stuck inside my head. It was not a pleasant place to be.

Way to ruin your life, Jake.

After what seemed like hours, Ms. Hardish walked over to me. And judging by the worried expression on her face, I must have looked pretty bad. "It's okay, Jake.

You can try again later," she said softly, then took me by the hand and helped me through the aisle.

Dean said "Choke!" under his breath as we walked past his desk. He just couldn't resist the urge to make fun of me. He couldn't resist the urge to make fun of anyone, ever.

"Dean!" Ms. Hardish snapped. "I'll see you after class."

"It's just a joke," he said. "Sheesh, lighten up already."

I collapsed into my seat and put my head in my hands.

No doubt about it. Worst. Day. Ever.

To read what happens next, order your copy of *Jake Murphy and the Karate Choke* today.

END NOTES

Jake Murphy and the Karate Choke is available now at
www.amazon.com/dp/1999232232

Thank you again for reading *Siarra Jones Skating Into Trouble*. If you enjoyed it, please consider leaving a review to help others discover my writing.
It really makes a difference.

Sincerely,
Paul Breau

ALSO BY PAUL BREAU

Step-by-Step series

Siarra Jones: Skating Into Trouble
Jake Murphy: The Karate Choke
Friendship or Fame: Mia Finds Her Voice

ABOUT THE AUTHOR

Paul Breau lives in Vancouver, British Columbia, Canada. He writes coming of age, middle grade stories that feature smart, funny, and authentic characters dealing with challenging situations.
Paul lives with his wife, daughter, and a Chihuahua dog named Poppy. He loves skating, karate, and lots of other sports. He is an avid reader and loves to draw.

Paul completed a BA in English Literature from the University of British Columbia.

If you enjoy Paul's books, the best way to keep up with his work is to join the Paul Breau reader list at PaulBreau.com

Made in the USA
Columbia, SC
19 December 2023

29191803R00083